POWER
PLAY

BY JAKE MADDOX

text by
Jessica Gunderson

STONE ARCH BOOKS
a capstone imprint

Jake Maddox JV Girls books are published by
Stone Arch Books
a Capstone imprint
1710 Roe Crest Drive
North Mankato, Minnesota 56003

www.mycapstone.com

Library of Congress Cataloging-in-Publication Data

Names: Maddox, Jake, author. | Gunderson, Jessica, author.
Title: Power play / by Jake Maddox ; text by Jessica Gunderson.
Description: North Mankato, Minnesota : Stone Arch Books, a Capstone imprint,
  [2017] | Series: Jake Maddox JV girls | Summary: Ninth-grade hockey player
  Kyla Woodson is hoping to win a spot on the varsity team mid-season—but she
  has at least one serious rival for the coveted position, and her supressed anger over
  her parents recent divorce seems to keep getting in the way.
Identifiers: LCCN 2016014836| ISBN 9781496536730 (library binding) | ISBN
  9781496536778 (pbk.) | ISBN 9781496536815 (ebook pdf)
Subjects: LCSH: Hockey stories. | Competition (Psychology)—Juvenile fiction.
  | Stress (Psychology)—Juvenile fiction. | Anger—Juvenile fiction. |
  Children of divorced parents—Juvenile fiction. | Mothers and
  daughters—Juvenile fiction. | CYAC: Hockey—Fiction. | Competition
  (Psychology)—Fiction. | Stress (Psychology)—Fiction. | Anger—Fiction. |
  Divorce—Fiction. | Mothers and daughters—Fiction.
Classification: LCC PZ7.M25643 Pt 2017 | DDC 813.6 [Fic] —dc23
LC record available at https://lccn.loc.gov/2016014836

Art Director: Nathan Gassman
Designer: Kayla Rossow
Media Researcher: Morgan Walters
Production Specialist: Tori Abraham

Photo Credits:
Capstone Studio: Karon Dubke, Cover; Shutterstock: Aaron Amat, (basketball) 96,
Angie Makes, design element, cluckva, design element, Dan Kosmayer, (stick) 96,
Eky Studio, design element, irin-k, (soccer ball) 96, Lightspring, (volleyball) 96,
Vaclav Volrab, design element

Printed in the United States of America in Stevens Point, Wisconsin.
009622F16

TABLE OF CONTENTS

CHAPTER 1

VARSITY DREAMS

The hockey puck slammed into Kyla Woodson's stick. She glided across the ice, puck in her control. She could hear her opponents gaining on her, but she was too fast.

As Kyla neared the goal, she locked eyes with the goalie. The defenders were still trying to catch up. Now was her chance. All she had to do was aim and score.

"You've got it, Woodson!" a shout came from the stands.

Kyla tensed. Tom, her mom's new boyfriend, was here — again. Her eyes flicked away from the goal. It was just for a split second, but a split second was all it took.

Mackenzie Martin, Kyla's ultimate rival, dashed in and hooked her stick around the puck. She sent it spinning in the other direction.

Kyla heard a cheer as the puck sailed into the net. She groaned. She'd just let her opponent score. Worse, she'd just let *Mackenzie* score.

Coach Adams blew her whistle. "Nice play, Mac!" she called. "Gather round, team."

Kyla resisted the urge to smash her stick against the ice. Even though it was only practice, she'd failed. She'd had an easy shot, and she'd lost it.

It was all Tom's fault.

As she glided toward Coach Adams, Kyla heard Tom's voice again. "Keep your eye on the goal, Woodson!" he yelled.

Just pretend like he's not there, Kyla told herself.

This year was supposed to be one of the greatest years of Kyla's life. She'd always dreamed of playing in this rink, the home of the Walker Ice Storms. The Ice Storms were one of the best varsity teams in the state. Now that she was in high school, she could finally try out for the team.

But the year hadn't started out so well. At tryouts, the varsity coach, Coach Rafferty, had announced she wasn't recruiting any ninth grade players. "At least not until mid-season, after I see some JV games," Coach Rafferty had said. "If anyone stands out, I may consider it."

Kyla had been brokenhearted. She was stuck on the junior varsity team.

Kyla let out a heavy sigh as she joined her teammates in a huddle. Not making varsity was just another disappointment in a series of bad events. Six months ago, her parents had gotten divorced. Then they had sold the house she'd grown up in. Since the start of the school year, she'd been splitting her time between her mom's new house and her dad's apartment. Neither place felt like home.

And now her mom had a new boyfriend — Tom.

Kyla shot another glance into the stands, where Tom was waving and grinning. She rolled her eyes. Tom was quite possibly the most annoying person on earth. He loved hockey, and he asked her endless questions about her skills.

Normally Kyla loved to talk about her favorite sport, but not with Tom. Tom acted like a know-it-all. And ever since the start of the season, he had been coming to almost all her practices.

I'll never make varsity now, not with him around, she thought. *He's just a big distraction that'll mess up my game.*

Ana Gonzales, Kyla's friend and the team's starting goaltender, skated up to the huddle and scooted in next to Kyla. "Hey, Fire. Thought you had that one for sure," she said.

"Fire" was Kyla's hockey nickname. She'd earned it in little league because she'd skated so fast, it was like she was on fire.

Kyla tossed her head in Tom's direction. "I wish they'd lock the rink during practice," she muttered.

She hadn't meant for Coach Adams to hear, but Coach never missed a thing. "You have to keep your head in the game," she told Kyla. She looked around at the rest of the girls. "And that means everything. Eyes, nose, ears, all of it. Every *inch* of you has to be in the game. Right?"

Mackenzie immediately piped up, "Yes, Coach!" She shot a glance at Kyla, but Kyla looked away.

Mackenzie had been her number one rival for as long as Kyla could remember. They'd gone to different middle schools and had often played against each other on the ice.

Last season, Kyla's team, the Sundogs, had played against Mackenzie's Cougars for the middle school championship. Tied at zero and with only eight seconds left of the game, Kyla had gained command of the puck and headed for the goal. She'd launched a shot but came up with only thin air. Mackenzie had stolen the puck.

Kyla had swirled around just in time to see Mackenzie score the winning goal of the game. She would never forget that moment.

Coach Adams glanced at the clock. "Practice is over for today, but we still have a lot of work to do. See you tomorrow."

At that, Mackenzie whipped off her helmet and shook out her long blond hair. Mac was one of those girls who seemed to have it all — confidence, good looks, and popularity. She never faltered on the ice. She always wore a smile, and she always encouraged even the weakest players. Mackenzie was perfect.

Kyla's stomach swirled with jealousy whenever she was around her. Now, they were at the same high school, on the same JV team, both trying to catch Coach Rafferty's eye and make varsity.

I can't keep making mistakes if I want to make varsity, Kyla thought as she skated off the rink. *At least I have until mid-season to get my game together.*

CHAPTER 2

MULTIPLY YOUR CONCENTRATION

"You coming?" Ana asked. She and Kyla were the last girls left in the locker room after practice.

Kyla paused. Lately, she had been staying at the ice rink as long as possible. She never felt like going home. "What day is it?" she asked.

"Wednesday," Ana answered. "Why?"

Kyla sighed. "The day determines where I go, remember? Mondays and Wednesdays I'm at Mom's, and Tuesdays and Thursdays I'm at Dad's. The weekends switch. It's so confusing."

Kyla had to admit, though, both of her parents seemed happier in their new lives. They didn't argue anymore, and her mom seemed to really like Tom.

But my life feels like a mess, Kyla thought as she pulled on her jacket. *And now Mackenzie is skating circles around me out on the ice.*

"Why does Mac have to be so perfect?" Kyla said out loud.

Ana shrugged. "She's good. We're lucky to have her on our team. It's definitely better than having her as an opponent. Right?"

"I guess," Kyla muttered. "But she might not be on our team for long if she makes varsity."

"I'm glad *I* don't have to worry about varsity," said Ana. "No way does Coach Rafferty need another backup goalie. But you shouldn't worry about it, either. Either you'll make varsity, or you get to keep playing with me on JV. Win-win."

Kyla gave a halfhearted smile. "Yeah, I suppose," she said.

But as they headed for the door, Kyla couldn't help but worry. She wanted a spot on the varsity team more than anything. She needed at least one good thing in her life.

* * *

"Please pass the spaghetti," Kyla said. She was starving after practice and was already on to seconds.

"You know, Kyla, I was watching you out there today," Tom said. He reached for the pot of spaghetti, balanced it in his hands, and kept talking. "And I think you need to multiply your concentration."

"Multiply my concentration?" Kyla repeated. She felt her mom's eyes on her, but she couldn't keep the irritation out of her voice.

"You have to concentrate on the puck, obviously. But you also have to concentrate on the goal. And you always need to know where your opponents are. And your teammates." Tom grinned. "See? Concentration multiplied!"

"Please pass the spaghetti, *Coach*," Kyla said.

"How did your algebra test go today?" Mom broke in.

"A lot of multiplication," Kyla snapped, taking the pot from Tom. She scooped some spaghetti onto her plate and scarfed it down. "May I be excused?"

Without waiting for a reply, Kyla shoved off her chair and ran to her room. She didn't even try to start her homework. She just flopped onto her bed, pulled out her phone, and clicked on Ana's number.

"Hey!" Ana answered. "What's up?"

"Ugh, I just needed to vent. Tom was here for dinner again," Kyla explained.

"Again? Sounds like he's practically moving in," Ana said.

Kyla groaned. "I hope not. Mom's only been dating him for two months. But they seem pretty serious."

"So how did dinner go?" Ana asked. "Did Tom offer any helpful tips on your technique?"

Kyla rolled her eyes. "Of course he did, and they were *so* helpful. He is beyond annoying. Maybe I should ask if I can just stay at Dad's forever."

"That seems drastic," Ana said. "Maybe you could just talk to Tom and tell him how you feel."

"No way!" Kyla protested. "He wouldn't listen to a word I say. He'd be too busy thinking of ways to criticize my game."

"Well . . . how about talking to your mom?" Ana suggested.

"No, I don't want to make her feel bad," Kyla said. "But I'll be at Dad's tomorrow. Then I won't have to think about Tom. All I'll have to do is decide what I want on my pizza for our weekly movie night."

At that thought, Kyla's mood brightened. She couldn't wait to be eating pizza and watching a movie with her dad, escaping from all her worries about Tom and making varsity.

THREE CHANCES

The sun was just starting to peek over the horizon as Kyla eagerly jumped into her mom's van the next day. She was heading to her early morning practice. Even after yesterday's terrible scrimmage, Kyla was looking forward to getting back in the rink. Maybe today she could redeem herself.

As they drove, they passed the local outdoor ice pond. The early morning light glittered off its surface.

Mom sighed a little. "Remember when I taught you to skate out there?" she asked.

"I've *always* known how to skate, Mom," Kyla answered, grinning.

Most people assumed it was Kyla's dad who'd taught her to skate. But Dad could hardly glide a few feet on the ice without falling over. It had been all Mom.

"I love seeing you out on the ice," Mom said, pulling up in front of the ice arena. She paused. "Tom does too."

Kyla rolled her eyes as she reached for the door handle. "Bye, Mom."

"Go get 'em, Fire!" Mom called just before the door closed.

Kyla sighed. Why did Mom have to ruin the moment by mentioning Tom? Maybe she should take Ana's advice and talk to her mom. She had to do something before Tom ruined her whole hockey season.

After putting on her gear, Kyla walked into the cool arena. Then she noticed someone in the center of the rink, next to Coach Adams. It was Coach Rafferty, the varsity coach.

Kyla's heart pounded as fiercely as if she'd just speed-skated a mile. She waved at Ana and joined the team as they crowded around to hear what the varsity coach had to say.

"Ladies," Coach Rafferty began, "we've had some injuries on varsity. So I'm going to be recruiting a few new players earlier than expected."

Kyla's hammering heart stopped mid-thump.

Coach Rafferty scanned the girls' faces. "I'll be watching you all in action. Not in practice, but in games. I want to see you under pressure."

From where she stood, Kyla could see Mackenzie's face shining with excitement. *She probably already thinks she'll make the team*, Kyla thought.

"I'll be watching the next three games," Coach Rafferty continued, "starting with tomorrow's game against the Rockets. I'm looking to add one to three girls to the roster. Show me your skills, and you may just earn a spot on the team."

Kyla swallowed as the players broke from the huddle to start their warm-ups. She was excited but also nervous. She'd thought she had until mid-season to perfect her game. Now, she had just one day.

"You've got this, Fire!" a voice shouted from the stands.

Kyla turned to see Tom grinning and waving at her. She gave him a small, halfhearted wave, trying to resist the urge to roll her eyes.

"Looks like you have a super-fan!" Mackenzie chirped. She smiled at Kyla as she adjusted her gloves. "Good luck tomorrow."

"You too," Kyla muttered. She glanced back at Tom. To her horror, she saw him leaning over the glass and talking excitedly to Coach Adams. She couldn't hear what he was saying, but he was waving his arms and gesturing toward the goal.

Kyla skated in close. She was just in time to hear Coach Adams say, "I'll think about it, Mr . . . ?"

Oh no, Kyla thought. *What is he up to now?*

"Taylor. Tom Taylor," he replied. "I'm a family friend of Fire Woodson!"

Coach glanced at Kyla and turned back to Tom. "Like I said, I'll think about it, Mr. Taylor." The coach didn't seem pleased as she skated toward the center of the ice.

"I'm sorry!" Kyla nearly tripped over her skates as she chased after Coach Adams. "Don't listen to him. He's just . . . I'll try to keep him away from practice."

"Don't worry about it, Kyla," Coach said. "You just focus on your game. I've dealt with a lot of hockey dads before. I can handle it."

"He's not my dad," Kyla said, but Coach had already turned away.

CHAPTER 4

BEST WING ON THE TEAM

That morning's practice was intense. Everyone expected the upcoming game against the Rockets to be an easy win, but now the stakes were higher. Tomorrow, every girl who wanted to make varsity would have to show off her abilities. Tomorrow, every girl wanted to shine.

After Coach Rafferty left, Coach Adams had the team practice speed and stick-handling by sending each girl down the ice with a puck. The rest of the team had to chase her.

When it was Kyla's turn, she took to the ice with confidence. *They don't call me Fire for nothing,* she told herself.

Kyla zoomed down the ice. She could hear the pack of girls behind her, but she was too fast. She easily slammed the puck into the goal.

"Nice job, Fire!" the coach called. "Let's see that speed at tomorrow's game."

Kyla smiled and glanced into the stands. Tom was gone.

She felt a stab of disappointment. She'd wanted Tom to see how fast she was. Maybe then he would've congratulated her instead of criticizing her.

"Let's go over plays for the game," Coach Adams said. "Bethany, you'll be our starting center."

The team captain, Bethany Charles, nodded. She was a sophomore and played on both JV and varsity. She didn't get much playing time during varsity games, so Coach kept her on the JV team too.

"Mac," the coach continued, "you'll be starting tomorrow's game as right wing. Kyla, you'll be left wing."

Kyla wanted to do a triple loop in excitement. But her joy faded as Coach went over the plays. Every single play had Kyla on the assist and Mackenzie or Bethany scoring.

Kyla wanted to be set up to score at least once. "Can we change it up just a little, Coach?" she asked. "I'm fast. I can get to the goal before the defense even has time to blink."

Coach Adams lowered her clipboard and looked at Kyla. "I know everyone wants the glory, but we're a team. Every girl on the ice has a job to do."

"Right, Coach," Kyla said quickly. She could sense Coach's irritation. Between her big mouth and Tom's butting in, Kyla was definitely on Coach Adams's bad side.

* * *

After practice, the locker room buzzed with excited talk about tomorrow's game and Coach Rafferty's varsity recruitment. But Kyla didn't feel like joining in.

How am I supposed to catch Coach Rafferty's eye if all I'm doing is assisting? Kyla wondered.

All Kyla wanted right now was to get out of the locker room as fast as she could. She nudged Ana and nodded to the door. "Let's go," she said.

The two friends headed out. On the way, they passed Mackenzie, who stood at the mirror near the door, applying lip gloss.

"Are you excited, Mac?" Tamika Kroll asked as she joined Mackenzie at the mirror. "You're easily the best wing on our team. You'll make varsity for sure."

Her face turning red, Kyla tried to duck as she passed the girls. But she saw Mackenzie nudge Tamika and dip her head in Kyla's direction.

"Oh!" Tamika said, turning from the mirror. "Kyla, I didn't mean . . ."

Kyla stopped and looked at the girls. She could feel sweat starting to pulse from her skin.

"Of course you'll make varsity, Mackenzie," Kyla said, her voice tight. "And it looks like I'll be the one assisting you."

"I can talk to Coach Adams about the plays," Mackenzie said, flashing Kyla a wide, lip-glossed smile. "You should be set up to score at least once."

"Don't bother," Kyla told Mackenzie. "I'm happy to assist."

As she followed Ana out the door, Kyla heard Mackenzie say, "I would love to be a varsity Ice Storm. I've been dreaming of it since I was a little girl."

I have too, Kyla thought, giving the door a small kick. *But it's never going to happen if I'm stuck in your shadow.*

CHAPTER 5

PLAY CHANGE

At the next night's game, Kyla shifted her weight as she awaited the starting lineup call. She glanced over at Coach Rafferty, who was sitting on the players' bench with a clipboard and pen in hand. Kyla knew the coach would be studying every single play and movement the JV players made.

Kyla nervously tapped her stick on the ice as the announcer's voice boomed over the loudspeaker. "Next up, starting at left wing, Number 18, Kyla 'The Fire' Woodson!"

Kyla glided to the center of the rink and high-fived her teammates. She heard her mom scream, "Fire on the ice!"

Glancing over, Kyla spotted her mom and Tom in the first row behind the goal cage. Her dad hadn't been able to come. Although Dad wasn't that into sports, he still tried to make as many of her games as he could. But work sometimes kept him busy during the evening.

The stands were only partially filled, mostly with parents and friends of the team. It was nothing compared to the varsity games, which drew the big crowds. Kyla imagined what it would be like to play for a packed arena. The pep band would be blasting tunes. The whole arena would be energized.

Concentrate on the game, Kyla told herself. *Stop dreaming.*

Kyla skated into position at the left of the blue circle, ready for the face-off. When the puck dropped, Bethany fought hard for it, but the

Rockets center swiped it. She took off into Ice Storms territory.

Thankfully, the defense was ready. Before the puck had even crossed the blue line, Shay Gilz, a Storms defender, was on the Rockets player. She stole the puck out from under the opponent and carried it back over the center line.

Kyla sailed into position for the first play. Shay would spin to Bethany, who would then pass to Kyla. Kyla would fake out the goalie by pretending to shoot. But instead, she'd pass to Mackenzie. Mac would catch the goalie off guard and take the shot. The Rockets would be so dizzy from the fast action, they wouldn't know what hit them.

At least, that's how the play was supposed to work.

As Shay lobbed the puck to Bethany, Kyla skated to the left edge of the offensive zone. She tightened her grip on her stick and crouched, ready for the pass.

But Bethany didn't pass to Kyla. She slapped the puck straight to Mackenzie's stick, skipping Kyla altogether. Kyla blinked, stunned.

Mackenzie moved in for a shot, but the goalie was ready. She lunged to the side and knocked the puck backward.

Kyla zoomed in for the rebound, but Mackenzie had already rounded up the puck. She shot again. This time the puck slid right between the goalie's legs.

"Aaaand, goal!" the announcer cried.

The small home crowd cheered. Mackenzie waved her stick in the air, basking in the glory.

Kyla skated off the ice for the line change. The second forward line would now take the ice, giving the starting forwards a rest.

Kyla knew she should be happy about the goal, but she burned with anger. Bethany and Mackenzie had avoided passing to her, even though their three-person play was a sure shot.

Mackenzie had taken a chance, and she'd made a difficult goal. Coach Rafferty was sure to notice.

Kyla plopped down on the bench. She leaned over to hear what Coach Adams had to say about the play changeup as Mackenzie and Bethany filed in behind her. Coach definitely wouldn't be happy with the sudden change of plans.

But to Kyla's surprise, Coach wasn't angry. "Nice eye out there, Bethany," she said. "You knew Mackenzie was ready, so you went for it. Great shot, Mac!"

Even though Mackenzie could've missed, Kyla added to herself. She reluctantly slapped the girls' hands for a high five.

"Only thirty seconds in and we scored!" Mackenzie said breathlessly as she sat down next to Kyla.

"Nice job," Kyla said through tight lips.

"Hey, sorry about cutting you out of the play," Mackenzie said. "Next time!"

Kyla nodded but didn't say anything. She kept her eyes out on the ice, pretending to focus on the action.

With a minute to go in the first period, Tamika, who was the center on the second forward line, broke away from the defense and landed a goal. That brought the score to 2–0.

As the buzzer blared to signal the end of the first period, Kyla heard a familiar voice. It was Tom — again.

"Coach Adams!" he boomed, coming toward the players' bench. "I think you need to exploit your valuables."

Exploit your valuables? Kyla thought. *What language is he speaking?*

Tom leaned over the railing and said something Kyla couldn't make out. Coach stared straight ahead as if she couldn't hear him. Tom shrugged.

Go away, Kyla thought. *Please just go away.*

But he didn't go away. Instead, he moved down and started talking to Coach Rafferty.

Oh no. Not Coach Rafferty. Kyla ground her teeth. *If he ruins my chances, I'll —*

"Kyla!" Coach Adams called.

With a jolt, Kyla realized she was the only girl still on the bench. The others were skating away to the locker room. She bolted from her seat.

In the locker room, Coach went over the strategies and plays. Nothing had changed. Kyla was still set up to assist.

Kyla frowned. *Fine,* she thought, *I'll just do my best. And I won't let annoying Tom or perfect Mackenzie ruin my game.*

But as she left the locker room, Kyla couldn't help wondering if Coach Rafferty would even notice her.

CHAPTER 6

ATTACK OF THE MAC

The starters took the ice again at the beginning of the third period. Unfortunately, it didn't go any better for Kyla. In the middle of the period, Bethany assisted Mac again for the Storms' third goal.

Kyla huffed out a frustrated breath as the crowd cheered. Why was she was even on the ice if no one was ever going to pass to her?

After the goal, the Rockets center had control of the puck. She danced in front of Ana, waiting for her chance to shoot. Ana matched the girl's movements, parallel shuffling to protect the net.

The Rockets center finally slapped the puck, aiming over Ana's left shoulder. But the puck sailed over the net and was now swirling behind the goal.

Shay, a Storms defender, raced to retrieve the puck. She easily snatched it out from under one of the Rockets.

Kyla dodged a defender and zoomed toward Shay, who snapped the puck to her. Kyla zipped into the offensive zone. Tom's words popped into her brain — *exploit your valuables.*

Kyla's value was her speed. *I'm faster than any rocket*, she thought. *I'm on fire!*

She reached the goal before any other player had a chance to catch up. The Rockets goalie, though, was ready to pounce.

Just aim and shoot, Kyla told herself. *You can do it.*

Then she saw Mackenzie gliding up the far right of the rink. The goalie's eyes were still focused on Kyla. She didn't even notice Mac. Apparently she didn't know Tom's advice to multiply your concentration.

Kyla hesitated. She could try for a shot but risk missing. Or she could pass to Mac, who would have a better chance of a goal. And no matter what choice she made, Coach Rafferty would be watching.

With a deep breath, Kyla shot the puck to Mackenzie. She couldn't risk missing the shot and looking like a bad team player in front of the varsity coach.

Mackenzie received the pass and immediately flicked her wrist, sending the puck flying. It slammed into the net. Score!

Kyla heard her name over the loudspeaker: "Kyla Woodson with the assist. And Mackenzie Martin for her third goal of the game! Ladies and gentlemen, that's a hat trick!"

Kyla groaned. She'd just helped Mackenzie score her first hat trick of the season.

Back on the bench, Kyla tried not to listen as her teammates congratulated Mackenzie.

"You know what this means, Mac!" Bethany exclaimed. "You get to wear the Hat to Pizza Pizzazz tonight!"

Kyla had forgotten all about the Hat, a tradition for Walker hockey teams. Any girl who scored a hat trick — three goals in one game — wore the Hat to after-game celebrations and to the next school day. The Hat itself was a little silly — the blades of two hockey sticks poked from the top like horns and three pucks were glued to the front — but to wear it was an honor.

Since hat tricks were hard to make, it wasn't too often the Hat made an appearance. Everyone always crowded around the Hat girl.

Tonight, Mackenzie had for sure impressed Coach Rafferty. Now she would also be the star at Pizza Pizzazz.

All thanks to my assist, Kyla thought miserably.

CHAPTER 7

MARAUDER MADNESS

On Tuesday afternoon, Kyla spotted her mom's van in the school parking lot. The Ice Storms had won their game against the Rockets 5–0, and now they were ready to try for another victory against the Moss Lake Marauders today. Since Moss Lake was only a town over, parents were driving the players to the away game.

Kyla's stomach twitched with a combination of nerves and excitement. It was her second chance to show Coach Rafferty what she could do.

As Kyla was about to hop into her usual place in the front seat, she froze. Tom was sitting there, waving.

Kyla groaned. Why did Tom have to be here? She'd wanted to spend the drive gearing up for the game and listening to the new playlist she'd made.

Last season, whenever her mom drove her across town to games, they'd blared Kyla's game playlist. They had a ritual. Now Tom had broken it.

"Fire!" Tom greeted her as she slid into the backseat. "Ready to heat up the ice?"

"Mm-hmm," Kyla answered. She gave her mom a glare in the rearview mirror.

"I invited Tom to tag along," Mom said. "He was going to meet me there, but this saves on gas."

"Do you need some gas money, Tom?" Kyla asked. "I have some money I earned from babysitting that I could give you."

A tense silence fell over the van. Kyla caught her mom's eye again in the mirror and knew she'd be in trouble later. Mom did not like any mouthing off.

"So," Tom said, breaking the silence, "I called Coach Adams the other day."

Sweat broke out on Kyla's neck. "What?" she said. "You called? Why? What did you say?"

"I had a great idea on how you could get more playing time," Tom answered.

"Oh, really?" Kyla couldn't keep the sarcasm out of her voice, even though her mom was eyeing her in the mirror again.

"I told her to switch out the center, Number 77. Bethany something? I suggested she play you as the center."

"Why would you do that?" Kyla snapped. "I like playing wing."

"You need to show the coach you're versatile," Tom said. "You'd make a great center. And you'd still play wing, but on the second forward line. So you'd be out on the ice twice as much."

"That's not how it works, Tom," Kyla informed him. "Mackenzie, Bethany, and I are the starting forward line. We work well together. We're not changing!" Kyla felt her voice rising. "Do you know *anything*? Have you ever even played hockey?"

"Kyla!" Her mom's voice was stern. "Tom's just trying to —"

"I don't care," Kyla interrupted. She popped in her earbuds and turned on her playlist, dialing the volume up to drown out everything else.

Turning her eyes to the window, Kyla watched the trees whipping past. She was glad she'd be riding home with her dad tonight.

* * *

Kyla tried to forget about what had happened with Tom, but she couldn't hold it in when she saw Ana in the locker room.

"He actually told Coach Adams to change up the starting line," Kyla said. "Can you believe it?" She slammed her bag down with emphasis. "What is he going to do next?"

"Yikes. He's like a ticking Tom-bomb," Ana joked. "You never know when he'll go off."

Just then Coach Adams walked into the locker room. "We're doing a little switch-a-roo of the forward lines tonight," she announced.

Kyla's heart pounded. *A switch?* she thought.

"Tamika, you'll replace Kyla as starting left wing. Kyla, you'll play center on the second forward line."

Kyla swallowed. She couldn't believe she'd been removed as a starter! Despite her recent slip-ups, she was still one of the best players on the team.

This has to be Tom's doing, she thought angrily. *Coach is getting revenge for Tom butting in.*

"Coach Adams," Kyla blurted out. "We haven't even practiced the new lineup. Are you sure we —"

"Of course I'm sure!" Coach Adams said. "Practice the new forward lines during warm-up."

Out on the rink, Kyla skated to Ali Donalds and Mandi Thomas, the two wings of the second forward line. They practiced passing as the warm-up clock ticked down. Kyla couldn't help but watch as Mackenzie, Bethany, and Tamika easily slapped pucks back and forth. It was as if they'd been playing together for ages.

Kyla passed to Ali. Ali missed, and the puck flew by her. She scrambled after it.

Mackenzie wouldn't have missed, Kyla thought with a sigh. *I might actually miss playing with her.*

Now, she was stuck with two girls who weren't as skilled. She'd really have to shine if she wanted to impress Coach Rafferty.

I can't mess this up, Kyla thought.

* * *

Marauders fans filled the home section at the start of the game. The announcer called the starting lineup, and Kyla could hardly bear to watch when Tamika skated into the place she'd once held.

From the stands, a voice that sounded suspiciously like Tom's shouted, "Where's the Fire?"

Thanks, Tom, Kyla thought as she skated to the bench. *Way to make it worse.*

The ref dropped the puck at center. In no time at all, Bethany shot to Mackenzie, who sent the disc sailing into the net. The goal horn blared.

Kyla cheered halfheartedly. Once again, Mackenzie had scored within the first minute of the game. Kyla glanced over at Coach Rafferty, who was sitting at the far end of the bench. The coach was scribbling something onto her clipboard.

At the next line change, Kyla skated onto the ice to take her new position as center. The Marauders center, Number 9, crouched in front of her as they waited for the puck to drop. She held her stick tight like a weapon and stared Kyla down.

"Better watch out," the girl snarled. "By the end of the game, the Zamboni will be wiping the Ice Storms off the ice."

Kyla glared back at her opponent. *So that's how the Marauders play,* she thought.

The ref skated into place, puck in hand. Kyla snapped the puck to Ali before the other center even realized it had dropped.

Ali skated across the blue line and hesitated. Kyla zoomed past her, wide open for the pass. Ali knocked the puck to Kyla's stick.

Suddenly Kyla was flat on her back, her legs flailing and her stick in the air. She lay on the ice for a second, stunned. She hadn't even seen a defender coming toward her.

FWEEEET! The ref's whistle shrieked. Kyla scrambled to her feet.

"Penalty! Marauders Number 22, for tripping. Ice Storms Number 18, for slashing. Minor penalties, two minutes each."

Slashing? Kyla thought, furious. *Unbelievable.* She'd just been trying to hold onto her stick when Number 22 tripped her.

Kyla felt the arena's eyes on her as she skated to the penalty box. She slammed the door shut.

The next two minutes felt like the longest minutes of Kyla's life. Marauders fans, excited by the penalties, screamed and pounded on the glass.

Ali and Mandi passed the puck back and forth in front of the goal. Neither girl tried to take a shot.

Kyla could hardly watch. If she hadn't gotten a penalty, the Ice Storms would have had a five-on-four power play. Kyla could've scored easily. Instead she was stuck in the box with a penalty that she didn't deserve.

One minute into the penalty, a Marauder slammed the puck past Ana and into the net. The home crowd went wild and screamed, "Sieve! Sieve! Sieve!" at Ana.

It's all my fault, Kyla thought. *I should've been paying more attention to Number 22.*

Tom's words floated into her brain. *Multiply your concentration.*

"Shut up, Tom," Kyla muttered to herself. "Just shut it."

CHAPTER 8

ICE RINK MELTDOWN

The second period flew by as the teams went back and forth across the ice. No one scored. Not even Mackenzie could sneak a shot into the net.

Kyla felt dizzy and exhausted from chasing the puck. She heavily huffed in and out. Her building frustration was making it even harder to breathe. By the end of the period, the score was still tied at 1–1.

The third period didn't start out any better. Thirty seconds in, Tamika missed a drop pass from Mackenzie. By the time Tamika realized she'd skated past the puck, the Marauders had scooped it away.

"Adams!" a voice shouted above the noisy crowd.

Kyla didn't have to turn to see who was yelling. It was Tom.

Tom charged down from the stands. "Put Fire on the ice!" he cried.

Kyla glanced at Coach Adams. The coach sat as rigid as if she'd been frozen in place.

"It's all your fault, Tom," Kyla hissed quietly to herself.

At the next line change, Kyla's heart was still pounding in fury. She'd been removed as starter and was playing a position she didn't want. She'd gotten an unfair penalty. And now Tom was butting in — again. She skated onto the ice, trying to shake off her anger.

In the defensive zone, the Marauders took a shot and missed. A Storms defender came up with the rebound and passed to Ali.

In a flash, Number 22 charged after her. As the two grappled along the boards, Kyla saw the

Marauder's stick rise above her shoulders and connect with Ali's elbow.

FWEET! "Penalty on Marauders Number 22 for high-sticking!" the ref called.

Number 22 skated toward the penalty box. As she whizzed past Kyla, she stuck out her elbow and slammed Kyla in the shoulder.

"Unsportsmanlike conduct!" Kyla cried.

But the refs hadn't been watching. No penalty was called.

These Marauders play dirty, Kyla thought. *We have to win this game.*

"Power play, Ice Storms!" the announcer called.

Kyla gripped her stick as she skated into position for the face-off. *And this is our chance.*

Snagging the puck, Kyla slid it to Mandi. Mandi surged toward the goal but missed, and the Marauders picked up the rebound.

Ana held off the goal attempt, dropping to the ice and putting her knees together in a butterfly position. A Storms defender spun the puck to Kyla, and she took off as fast as she could.

Kyla whipped past the blue line. The goalie was caught off guard, surprised to see Kyla coming at her with such speed.

The goal was wide open. Kyla slid her bottom hand down the stick, brought the blade behind her back leg, swept her arm forward, and flicked the puck off the blade. A perfect wrist shot.

Except it wasn't perfect.

Ping! The puck hit the side of the cage and shot out into the stands. Kyla could only stare at the goal, totally stunned. The ref blew the whistle to stop play.

A deafening cheer rose from the Marauders fans at the missed shot. Kyla crouched forward, head in her hand, as the cheers rained down on her.

I missed, she thought, gasping to keep the sobs in her chest from breaking free. *I had a perfect chance, and I missed.*

Kyla lined up for the face-off, but she was still shaking from her missed attempt. The Marauders center took the puck easily.

"Be quicker on the draw!" she heard Tom shout.

Kyla tried to calm herself as she skated to the center line. *Maybe there will be another chance,* she thought, glancing at the clock. Twenty seconds left of the power play.

The Marauders took aim at the goal, but Ana knocked the puck out.

Five seconds left.

Ali gained control of the puck. She glanced around the ice, looking uncertain. Kyla skated into her view, ready for the pass.

Three, two, one.

Number 22 slid out of the penalty box and charged toward Kyla. "Nice shot, rubber wrists!" she teased.

Ali lobbed the puck in Kyla's direction. Number 22 swung her stick over Kyla's and hooked the puck.

"Gotcha, rubber wrists!" Number 22 taunted.

All Kyla's built-up rage hurtled through her like a volcano. *Stay calm,* said a tiny voice in her mind.

But her body didn't listen.

Kyla slammed Number 22 against the boards. The other girl threw down her stick, grabbed Kyla's shoulders, and whipped her around until both players fell onto the ice. Kyla spun onto her back, and the Marauders player fell on top of her.

Whistles screeched from all directions, but Number 22 was still gripping Kyla's shoulders and glaring down at her. She swished something around in her mouth.

She's going to spit on me! Kyla realized. She shoved the other girl off just as a long string of drool slipped onto Kyla's helmet.

Two refs pulled the girls apart. "Penalty, Number 18, for roughing!" one ref called.

Kyla was not surprised. As she got to her feet, she waited for the next penalty call. But none came.

"She threw me to the ice!" Kyla shouted to the ref. "And spit on me!"

But the ref's face remained solid. It was as if she hadn't heard a word Kyla said.

Number 22 grinned as Kyla slid past her toward the penalty box. "Aww, poor baby has to sit in the box!"

It was all Kyla could do to not shove the other girl down again. She gave the penalty box door a good kick and sank onto the seat. Her mind was spinning.

She hadn't had that kind of fight since she was in little league. Since then, Kyla had always played by the rules. She'd never let her emotions get to her — until now.

Kyla had just let her team down again. And she'd let herself down too.

She glanced over at Coach Rafferty on the bench. *I've definitely caught her attention now*, Kyla thought, *but for all the wrong reasons.*

CHAPTER 9

RIVALS

The Storms, outnumbered on the ice, fought off the Marauders as best they could. But the other team pounded off shots until one squeaked past Ana. The Marauders were up 2–1.

Kyla slid out of the penalty box, and Coach Adams motioned for a line change. "What were you doing out there, Woodson?" Coach said as Kyla hopped into the players' bench. "You know we don't play dirty."

"Number 22 has it out for me!" Kyla argued.

"That's no excuse," Coach told her. "If you can't keep your head in the game, you can sit on the bench."

Kyla sighed. When would she learn not to open her big mouth? "No, I want to help win this game!" she said.

"That's more like it," Coach said.

Kyla turned her attention to the game. Bethany shot the puck off to Tamika. Tamika passed to Mackenzie. Mac faked right, then left, and then launched a backhanded shot straight into the net.

Kyla clapped along with her teammates. She didn't care that it was Mackenzie who'd made the goal. The Ice Storms had just tied the game.

If we win, Kyla thought, *maybe everyone will forget about my lousy playing.*

* * *

Only twenty-five seconds remained in the third period. Kyla hopped off the boards for the next line change. She was determined to redeem herself.

When the Marauders gained control of the puck, Kyla raced across the center line. A Marauders player was charging down the ice toward the goal. The girl flicked the puck to a teammate on the right.

Kyla flew in front of the puck, intercepting the pass and stopping the Marauders drive. She shot to Ali, who aimed for a goal. She missed. Mandi recovered the puck and shot again — another miss.

The buzzer blared. The game had ended, 2–2.

"Nice save, Fire!" Mackenzie said as the team lined up to slap hands with the Marauders. "If you hadn't intercepted that pass, we could've lost!"

"We should've won," Kyla muttered, but Mackenzie had already turned away.

Inside the locker room, everyone was quiet. Sometimes a tie was worse than a loss. There were no clear winners or losers.

The locker room door swung open, and Coach Rafferty walked in. All the girls stopped what they were doing and turned toward the coach.

"I just wanted to congratulate you ladies on the game," she said. "It wasn't a win, but you never gave up." She looked over at Mackenzie and Tamika. "I saw some excellent teamwork and puck-handling tonight."

Kyla watched Mac's face light up with a big grin. Then Coach continued, locking eyes with Kyla. "There's also a lot of passion on this team. You need passion to be a great player, but you have to control it. Always remember to keep your cool."

Kyla felt her throat tighten. She could barely swallow as her cheeks turned red.

Coach Rafferty scanned the room again. "I'll see you all again this Friday for one final game before I make my decision on varsity recruits. Good luck." With that, the coach left the room.

Ana turned to Kyla. "So, sounds like Mac is in the running for a spot on varsity, huh?" she whispered.

"There's no question about it," Kyla said, her face still hot with embarrassment. "It's a definite."

"Don't worry," Ana said. "There's still one more game to prove yourself."

"What's the point? I'll never be as good as Mac," Kyla said, her voice rising. "She never misses a goal. She never screws up. She never gets a penalty."

Ana shook her head. "Kyla . . ." she began.

But Kyla continued, unable to stop. "Mac doesn't have to deal with someone like Tom. She doesn't have to bounce between Mom's house and Dad's house. Mac's life is perfect. Mac is perfect!"

Too late, Kyla realized all her teammates were staring at her. Ana was staring too, but her eyes looked past Kyla's shoulder.

Kyla slowly turned around. Mackenzie stood behind her, her face red and her jaw clenched. "What is this about, Kyla?" she snapped.

Although a small part of Kyla knew she should apologize, her rage was still swirling. "Well, it's true, isn't? You are a perfect hockey player."

Mackenzie sighed. "You know, all those years we played against each other, I couldn't wait to be on the same team as you. I knew we'd make a great forward line."

Kyla opened her mouth to speak, but nothing came out.

"But apparently you think we're still rivals," Mackenzie said, crossing her arms.

"I don't, I —" Kyla started. She searched for the right words to say. "I just really wanted to make varsity. And I screwed it up."

Mackenzie raised an eyebrow. "It was one bad game. So what? You still have a good chance of making varsity. You're an awesome player."

"You're just saying that," Kyla mumbled. She knew Mac always encouraged everyone, even the weak players.

But Mackenzie shook her head. "Seriously," she insisted. "I'd give anything to have your speed on the ice. I've been jealous of your skating skills since forever."

Kyla gave a small laugh. "Wow, that's a long time." She couldn't believe Mac had been jealous of her too.

"And I'm not perfect, by the way," Mackenzie went on. "You should've seen the checking penalty I got in seventh grade. It cost my team the game!"

"Really?" Kyla asked.

Mackenzie shuddered. "I don't even want to think about it."

"I know the feeling," Kyla admitted. She glanced around and realized the locker room had emptied. Ana stood by the door, waiting.

Kyla picked up her bag, not knowing what

to say next. "Well, um, thanks, Mac. And sorry I freaked out at you. See you tomorrow?"

Mac beamed at her. "Just bring the Fire back at our next game, and we'll call it even. See ya!"

Kyla let out a long breath. Maybe now she could forget about trying to beat Mackenzie and focus on doing her best and helping the team. She joined Ana by the locker room door.

"Wow, how did that go?" Ana asked as they started walking.

"Better than I expected," Kyla admitted. "I guess it is dumb to think of a teammate as a rival. There's been so much going on lately — I just lost it. I think we're good now, though."

As the girls neared the front door of the arena, Kyla heard Tom calling her name. He jogged up, and Kyla froze. All the relief she'd felt after talking to Mackenzie faded.

"Hey, you got a raw deal on that penalty. I don't know what that ref was thinking, not calling anything on Number 22, but I was thinking you could —" Tom began.

Kyla spotted her dad waiting for her. "Sorry, gotta go!" she said, not letting Tom finish. She waved goodbye to Ana and sprinted toward her dad.

"Hey, Fire! Good game," Dad said, giving her a tight hug. "So, uh . . . why did you have to sit in the penalty box?"

Kyla laughed. Even after all her years of hockey, her dad was still fuzzy on the rules. She explained the penalties to him as she followed him to his car. As she climbed in, Kyla asked, "Hey, Dad? Do you want to listen to the new playlist I made?"

"Sure, kiddo!" Dad answered. "Hook it up!"

Kyla grinned and started blasting the music. *Mac was right — tonight was just one bad game*, she told herself. *Tomorrow will be a better day.*

CHAPTER 10

THE ICE POND

With how she had mouthed off to Tom on
the way to the Marauders game the day before,
Kyla was sure her mom would ground her. But
when Kyla got home from school on Wednesday
afternoon, Mom didn't say a word about it.

Kyla went to her room, opened her laptop,
and started on her homework. But she couldn't
concentrate on any of it. Her frustration about Tom
had been eating her up inside. It was affecting her
game, and it was affecting her relationship with
her mom.

She had to stop holding back. She had to take charge.

Kyla went downstairs. She found her mom in the living room, reading a book.

"Hey, Mom?" Kyla started. "I want to talk to you about something."

Her mom looked up. "About Tom?" she guessed.

Kyla nodded.

"That's what I thought," Mom said with a sigh. "So Tom and I have decided it would be best if —"

"No!" Kyla broke in. "Don't break up just because of me!"

"No, that's not it," Mom said quickly. "We've decided he should stay away from your games and practices for a while."

Kyla let out a breath and nodded. "It would be nice if he didn't come to all my practices," she admitted. Then she paused. "But I don't mind that he comes to my games. Not really. I just don't want him talking to the coaches, or trying to give me so much advice. I want to play without him interfering all the time. If he can do that, we'll be good."

"He does get a bit overenthusiastic," Mom agreed.

Kyla sighed, thankful her mom understood. "He's like an armchair quarterback. You know, the kind who think they know everything but have never even stepped foot on the field."

Mom's smile faded. "Maybe you should talk to him," she said.

Kyla chewed her lip. "I . . . I wouldn't know what to say. Can't you just tell him?"

"I think you need to talk to him," Mom answered. "Who knows? You might be surprised by how much you have in common."

* * *

Thursday morning, Kyla woke early and stared out her window at the lightening sky. She didn't have practice until after school, but her legs itched to get out on the ice.

Kyla scribbled a note to her mom. *At the pond for a quick skate. Have my phone. Will be back soon.*

After grabbing her skates, she walked the few blocks to the pond. It was nearly empty — there was only one skater slowly gliding in big circles on the north end.

Kyla laced up her skates and stepped onto the ice. She'd just stay at the south end, out of the other person's way. She started skating small laps.

This feels so good, Kyla thought. *Just being on my skates. Sometimes I wish I had skates for feet!* She giggled aloud at that mental picture.

At her laughter, the other skater looked over. Their eyes met. It was Tom.

Kyla skidded to a stop. She'd had no idea Tom could skate. He'd never once mentioned it.

Tom gave a small wave and kept skating. But Kyla skated closer and waited in the middle of the pond for him to make another lap. As he neared her, she held out her hand. "Hey, Tom!"

He came to a stop next to her. "Hey! Getting ready for tomorrow's game?" he asked.

"Yeah. Just clearing my head." Kyla gestured to his skates. "I didn't know you skated."

Tom nodded. "I come out here every morning before work. It's a great way to start the day."

"Definitely!" Kyla agreed. "Do you ever skate with my mom?"

Tom laughed. "No, she'd probably skate circles around me. I'm not that great anymore."

"Anymore?" Kyla asked.

Tom was silent for a moment. Then he sighed. "I was the starting center on my high school team up until senior year. I'm lucky I still have all my teeth!" He forced a laugh. "I had a college scholarship in the works. My big dream was to play for the NHL. Now I'm an accountant instead."

Kyla frowned. "What happened senior year?"

"I tore my ACL. First game of the season too. Lost my scholarship. Lost my dream . . ." Tom's voice sounded pained, and he trailed off. Then he shook his head quickly. "It's all in the past, though."

Kyla was speechless for a moment. "Why didn't you tell me?" she asked.

"Honestly, I tried to forget all about hockey," Tom replied. "But then I saw you play. You have the same drive I once had."

Kyla was silent for a second. "Maybe you could give me some tips," she said slowly. Tom opened his mouth to speak, but Kyla quickly went on. "But not with words. Actually show me, out here on the ice."

"Well, I suppose I could dig out my old hockey stick," Tom said. "There's this great play we used at the championship game my junior year . . ."

As Tom went on excitedly, Kyla couldn't help but roll her eyes while she grinned. He was still the same Tom. But somehow talking to him, knowing he'd played hockey, made him not quite as annoying.

"One more thing," Kyla said when he'd finally stopped talking. "I don't need you giving me advice *all* the time, though. It gets old. And please don't talk to the coaches about me. I don't think they like it. I don't, either."

Tom sighed. "I have so many opinions! Sorry, I know I have a big mouth. I'll try to shut it."

"I've got a big mouth sometimes too," Kyla told him. "So, see you at tomorrow's game?"

Tom smiled. "Only if you want me there," he said.

Kyla smiled back. She knew that her mom loved Tom and that he was a part of her life. It was time to accept it and give Tom a chance. Or at least try. "I definitely do," she said.

CHAPTER 11

BRINGING THE FIRE

"Starting at left wing, Number 18, Kyla 'The Fire' Woodson!"

Kyla skated to the center line and slapped her teammates' hands. She was back on the forward line with Mackenzie and Bethany, the way it should be.

A loud cheer burst from the stands. Kyla glanced over to see her mom and Tom, waving wildly. Her dad sat next to them, giving her a big smile and thumbs up.

Tonight was Kyla's last chance to show Coach Rafferty that she was cut out for the varsity team. She vowed to skate her best and focus on one play at a time. The Fire was back.

It wasn't going to be an easy game, though. The Comets defense had a reputation for being fast, and they were excellent stick handlers. The Ice Storms forwards would have to work their hardest to make any goals.

"Offensive line, you need to be on the lookout," Coach Adams reminded the girls as they gathered around her for the pre-game pep talk.

"We will, Coach," Kyla said. She caught Mackenzie's eye. Mac gave her a smile and a nod. They were both ready to tear up the ice.

The two teams got into place for the starting face-off. The puck dropped. Bethany instantly grabbed it and sent the puck flying across the ice to Kyla.

Kyla moved to the left edge of the rink. A defender trailed close behind. Suddenly, the other girl came up on Kyla's right and pushed her into the boards.

Hold on to the puck. Stay focused, Kyla told herself as the defender's stick jammed against hers.

Tightening her grip, Kyla pressed her right elbow against the defender to keep her back. Then, in one swift movement, she twisted her body and spun away from her opponent. She sailed away, puck still in her control.

Kyla heard the cheers of the Ice Storms crowd as they saw her come away with the puck. Curving around the back of the goal cage, she brought the puck in front of the goal. She could see Mackenzie skating up behind her.

Just then, Kyla spotted a Comets defender coming up on her left. She lifted her stick just slightly and zoomed forward, leaving the puck behind for a drop pass.

Mackenzie didn't miss a beat. She snatched up Kyla's pass, quickly launching the puck into the net. The goal siren blared.

As the announcer called her name on the assist, Kyla heard Tom shout, "Look out for the Fire!"

Kyla raised her stick and grinned. The Ice Storms were up 1–0.

Let's keep it that way, she thought.

* * *

At the beginning of the second period, the Comets were fired up. They were fighting hard to even the score. Two minutes in, the Comets already had six shots on goal. Ana knocked each one back.

But in the final few minutes of the period, a Comets forward charged the goal and made a powerful slapshot. The puck flew past Ana. The teams were now tied 1–1.

In the locker room between second and third periods, Coach Adams gathered the girls around.

"I don't want another tied game, Ice Storms,"
she told them. "We have to keep our heads in the
game, and go for the win!

Kyla wiped the sweat from her forehead and
focused on Coach Adams's words. Her legs ached,
but she knew she needed to keep giving it her all
during the third period.

As the girls filed back into the rink, Kyla
realized she'd hardly given Coach Rafferty a
thought throughout the game — or Tom for that
matter. Her head had been where it should have
been all along — in the game.

Kyla nudged Ana's shoulder as they took
the ice. "Keep up the saves, Gonzales," she said,
grinning at her friend.

"And keep dodging the defense, Woodson,"
Ana replied. "We can win this."

"No," Kyla said. "We *will* win this."

* * *

Both teams came out of the break feeling energized, and the third period ticked by with lots of back-and-forth action. But no one was scoring.

Kyla sat on the bench. She drummed her fists on her knees as she watched Tamika, Ali, and Mandi fight to make a goal. But the Comets defense was staying strong.

I need to be out there, Kyla thought.

With a minute to go, Kyla got her wish. Coach Adams called for a final line change.

Kyla immediately leaped from the bench and over the boards. *A minute to win it*, she thought, racing across the ice to the action.

A Comets offensive player was moving the puck along the boards near the center line. Shay zoomed in for the defense. She slapped the puck away from the Comets offense and launched it across the ice.

The puck skittered across the blue line into the offensive zone. It was a dump-and-chase play.

Shay had dumped the puck into Comets territory, and now the Storms attackers had to chase it.

Kyla went for it. She pumped her legs hard, skating faster than she ever had before. She reached the puck and brought it before the goaltender, who was waiting on high alert.

Multiply your concentration. Tom's words echoed in her brain. Kyla knew the goalie was ready. And she knew Mackenzie was coming up on her right.

Kyla slapped the puck to Mackenzie and skated left. Mac knocked the puck back to her. Before she even had time to think, Kyla caught the puck and sent it sailing into the right corner of the net. Goal!

"Yes!" Kyla shouted. She held up her stick in triumph as the goal siren blared and the crowd cheered.

Mackenzie rushed toward her and caught her in a spinning hug. "See? I knew we'd make a great team!" Mac exclaimed, panting for breath.

Kyla laughed. "We do!" she agreed.

As the announcer called her name for the goal, Kyla glanced into the stands, where her parents and Tom sat. Her dad high-fived her mom, and then he high-fived Tom too. Kyla gave them all a big grin before focusing back on the game.

In the final seconds, the Comets pulled their goalie and subbed in another attacker. But even with the extra player, they couldn't score a goal.

The buzzer blared, signaling the end of the game. The Ice Storms piled onto the ice. "Great goal, Fire!" the girls shouted as they crowded around her.

Ana almost tackled Kyla with a hug. "You were amazing!"

"Thanks! You too!" Kyla shouted above all the noise. She was both beaming and blushing under the attention from all her teammates.

But someone was missing. Kyla looked around for Mac. She spotted her at the edge of the rink, standing with Coach Rafferty. Just then, the coach looked up and saw Kyla. She waved her over.

Ana noticed Coach Rafferty too. She smiled and gave Kyla a nudge. "Go get 'em, Fire."

Kyla's heart thumped loudly, but this time it wasn't just from being completely exhausted. She felt like she was skating on air as she made her way to the coach.

Kyla skidded to a stop next to Mac. The teammates exchanged excited grins, then turned toward the coach.

"That was a great game, Kyla," Coach Rafferty started. "Way to use that passion."

"Thanks, Coach," Kyla replied breathlessly. Her tired legs shook as she waited for Coach Rafferty to continue.

The coach looked at both players and grinned. "Now, I wanted to talk to you two ladies about varsity . . ."

ABOUT the AUTHOR

Jessica Gunderson grew up in the small town of Washburn, North Dakota. She has a bachelor's degree from the University of North Dakota and an MFA in Creative Writing from Minnesota State University, Mankato. She has written more than fifty books for young readers. Her book *Ropes of Revolution* won the 2008 Moonbeam Award for best graphic novel. She currently lives in Madison, Wisconsin, with her husband and cat.

GLOSSARY

assist (uh-SIST) — to help and to make it easier for someone to do something; in sports, a pass that leads to a score by a teammate

concentrate (KAHN-suhn-trayt) — to focus your thoughts and attention on something

criticize (KRIT-uh-size) — to talk about problems in something or someone

drastic (DRASS-tik) — extreme or over-the-top action

intercepting (in-tur-SEPT-ing) — receiving a pass meant for an opposing player

recruiting (ri-KROOT-ing) — finding people with the right skills and asking them to join your group

redeem (ri-DEEM) — to make up for past mistakes

ritual (RICH-oo-uhl) — an action that is always performed in the same way and that has special meaning to the person doing it

versatile (VUR-suh-tuhl) — skilled and talented in many ways

DISCUSSION QUESTIONS

1. In your own words, discuss the different events that were happening in Kyla's life. How did they make Kyla feel? What in the text makes you think that?

2. When Kyla and Mackenzie started playing like teammates, they became a powerful offensive line. Talk about a time when you accomplished something great by working with others.

3. The ending to this story is a little open-ended, which means the author doesn't tell you exactly what happened. What do you think Coach Rafferty is about to say to Kyla and Mac? Why do you think the author chose to end this way?

WRITING PROMPTS

1. During the Marauders' game, Kyla had a tough time keeping her temper in check. Write a list of ten things that Kyla could've done to deal with her frustration in a healthy way. What did she actually do later in the story to solve her anger issue?

2. Write a paragraph that describes the relationship between Kyla and Mac at the beginning of the story. Then write a second paragraph that describes their relationship at the end. What caused the change?

3. At first, Kyla didn't want to talk to Tom, but when she finally did, she felt a lot better. Write a paragraph that summarizes what she learned during their conversation. How did this info help her understand Tom?

MORE ABOUT
ICE HOCKEY

Ice hockey may have developed from **stick and ball games** played in Great Britain in the 1700s. When immigrants came to North America, they started playing their games on the ice during the winter. Eventually the rules changed enough to form a new game — ice hockey!

The first indoor ice hockey game was played in **Montreal, Canada**, in 1875.

The **Seattle Vamps** were one of the first organized women's teams in the United States. They formed in 1916 and played against Canadian female teams.

Women's ice hockey first became part of the **Winter Olympic Games** in 1998. (Men's ice hockey became an Olympic sport in 1920.) That year, the United States won gold, Canada won silver, and Finland won bronze.

If players break the rules, the referee calls a **penalty**. A penalty often results in the player spending time in the penalty box. Some common penalties are:

Tripping — using the stick, arm, or leg to trip an opponent

Slashing — swinging the stick at an opponent

Roughing — shoving another player after the whistle has blown or away from the play

High-sticking — carrying the stick above the shoulders or the stick making contact above the shoulders of an opponent

Sometimes fans chant **"sieve!"** at the other team's goaltender when a shot gets through to the net. A sieve is a type of strainer made of wire mesh that liquid can pour through. Hockey fans say "sieve" to intimidate and throw off the goalie's concentration.

Men's hockey and women's hockey have similar rules. The main difference is that **body checking** is not allowed in women's hockey and results in a penalty. Body checking is when a player uses their body to separate an opponent from the puck.